AFRICAN PROVERBS

For All Ages

To my grandchildren, Hollis Abigail Cole and Miles Alexander Cole. Enjoy, learn from, and grow wiser as you read and think about the meaning of each of these African proverbs. —JBC

*To Harris, Lauren, Casey, and youngsters everywhere.
Get ready to think, to question, and to dream! —NL*

Published by Roaring Brook Press
Roaring Brook Press is a division of Holtzbrinck Publishing Holdings Limited Partnership
120 Broadway, New York, NY 10271
mackids.com

Prologue text copyright © 2021 by Johnnetta Betsch Cole
Illustrations copyright © 2021 by Nelda LaTeef
Map courtesy Shutterstock Images / Aliaksei Tarasau

Library of Congress Cataloging-in-Publication Data
Names: Cole, Johnnetta B., compiler. | LaTeef, Nelda, 1958- compiler, illustrator.
Title: African Proverbs For All Ages / collected by Johnnetta Betsch Cole
and Nelda LaTeef ; illustrated by Nelda LaTeef.
Description: First edition. | New York : Roaring Brook Press, 2021. |
Audience: Ages 4 to 8 | Audience: Grades 2–3 | Summary: "It has been
said that a proverb is a short sentence based on long experience.
African Proverbs is An Oprah Book about the power of proverbs, how they
evolve over time, and the wisdom of various cultures in Africa. Whether
you're young or old, proverbs can open your mind to new ways of seeing
the world. We underestimate children, assuming they are incapable of
understanding metaphor and deeper meaning. Children learn in multiple
ways, but for each method by which they learn, they need engaged
imagination and ignited visual sensibilities. And as adults, we
underestimate ourselves when we allow our lives to be about practical
matters only. Proverbs can stir our soul and spark our imagination"— Provided by publisher.
Identifiers: LCCN 2021011861 | ISBN 9781250756060 (hardcover)
Subjects: LCSH: Proverbs, African—Juvenile literature.
Classification: LCC PN6519.A6 C65 2021 | DDC 398.9096—dc23
LC record available at https://lccn.loc.gov/2021011861

Our books may be purchased in bulk for promotional, educational, or business use. Please contact your local bookseller or the
Macmillan Corporate and Premium Sales Department at (800) 221-7945 ext. 5442 or by email at MacmillanSpecialMarkets@macmillan.com.

First edition, 2021 • Book design by Jen Keenan
The illustrations for this book were created with acrylic, Indian ink, and collage on art board.
Printed in China by RR Donnelley Asia Printing Solutions Ltd., Dongguan City, Guangdong Province

1 3 5 7 9 10 8 6 4 2

AFRICAN PROVERBS

For All Ages

collected by
Johnnetta Betsch Cole
and **Nelda LaTeef**

illustrated by
Nelda LaTeef

New York

Acknowledgments

Illustrating *African Proverbs For All Ages* has been a joyful experience, not only because of my love for African proverbs but for the opportunity to collaborate with my dear friend and co-collector, Johnnetta Cole, who brought her inimitable ebullience, academic rigor, and discerning eye to this exciting endeavor hatched over a cup of tea. As great admirers of Oprah Winfrey, it is a tremendous honor to have our book designated "An Oprah Book." Indeed, Ms. Winfrey's belief in this project has been a driving force in its publication. And now a toast to our dynamic team at Macmillan: Jennifer Besser, Jen Keenan, Aram Kim, and Luisa Beguiristain. Cheers and thank you!

—Nelda LaTeef

Prologue

It has been said that a proverb is a short sentence based on long experience.

Whether you are young or old, proverbs can open your mind to a whole new way of seeing the world. We shortchange our children when we assume they are incapable of understanding metaphor and deeper meaning. There are multiple ways that children learn, but for each method by which they learn, they need their imaginations engaged and their visual sensibilities ignited. And as adults, we shortchange ourselves when we allow our lives to be about practical matters only. Proverbs can stir our souls and spark our imaginations.

This book, drawn from the wisdom of the diverse cultures of Africa and stunningly illustrated by my friend and acclaimed artist and author Nelda LaTeef, fully engages children by presenting four proverbs with each illustration. Readers may then choose which proverb they believe best narrates the illustration. The book also invites children and adults to step into what are sometimes complex notions about life, relationships, identity, society, and the human condition. When words fail us, proverbs are a bridge between the adult and the child mind. They are a gateway to deeper connections and understanding.

There are no people without conversations. But with proverbs, every conversation is sure to be rich and memorable. As an anthropologist, I have witnessed how proverbs are used by individuals to warn, instruct, or advise.

Proverbs are drawn from the community well. No one person is the author of a proverb. In this book, we have culled proverbs from the various cultures of Africa, the continent from which we have all descended. Wherever possible, we have credited proverbs with their specific country of origin; when not possible, we have attributed them to the continent of Africa. In instances where the same proverb has multiple variations, we selected the most compelling version.

Readers may be reminded of sayings from their own cultures that offer the same teachings as the proverbs in this book, but with different words. In this way, proverbs are conveyors of insights that may be universally accepted as valid. There is an African saying, "A wise person who knows proverbs can reconcile difficulties." Where the language of the material world may fail, proverbs transcend our differences and remind us of our common humanity.

Proverbs can and do evolve as cultures transform. That is why Nelda and I encourage children to create and make drawings to illustrate their own proverbs and, in so doing, to have a deeper conversation with themselves and with the world in which they live.

—Johnnetta Betsch Cole, PhD

A. "There can be no peace without understanding."

B. "You always learn a lot more when you lose than when you win."

C. "A friend is someone you share the path with."

D. "There are no shortcuts to the top of the palm tree."

A. "When the leg does not walk, the stomach does not eat."

B. "A village without elders is like a well without water."

C. "A clear conscience makes a soft pillow."

D. "Only once you have carried your own water will you learn the value of every drop."

A. "A lamp is not valued in the afternoon, but it is valued at night."

B. "Wisdom is like a baobab tree; no one individual can embrace it."

C. "One who is carried on another's back does not appreciate how far off the town is."

D. "A family tie is like a tree; it can bend, but it cannot break."

C. "To one who does not know, a small garden is a forest."

D. "Life is like a shadow and a mist; it passes quickly by and is no more."

C. "Dance in the sun, but turn your back to the clouds."

D. "A roaring lion kills no game."

A. "Restless feet may walk into a snake pit."

B. "Until the lion has his own storyteller, the hunter will always have the best stories."

C. "Not everyone who chased the zebra caught it, but the one who caught the zebra chased it."

D. "When the mouse laughs at the cat, there is a hole nearby."

A. "Tomorrow belongs to the people who prepare for it today."

B. "A single bracelet does not jingle."

C. "Instruction in youth is like engraving in stone."

D. "It is not what you call me but what I answer to that matters."

D. "You cannot tell a hungry child you gave her food yesterday."

A. "Between true friends, even water drunk together is sweet enough."

B. "When spiderwebs unite, they can tie up a lion."

C. "Many hands make light work."

D. "Return to old watering holes for more than water:
friends and dreams are there to meet you."

A. "She who learns must teach and she who teaches must learn."

B. "The words of the elders become sweet one day."

C. "If you wish to move mountains tomorrow, you must start by lifting stones today."

$$64 \div 2 = 32 \qquad 6 \times 6 = 36$$
$$49 \div 7 = 7 \qquad 5 \times 5 = 25$$
$$108 \div 9 = 12 \qquad 8 \times 8 = 64$$
$$81 \div 3 = 27 \qquad 9 \times 9 = 81$$
$$144 \div 12 = 12 \qquad 7 \times 7 = 49$$

D. "What you help a child to love can be more important than what you help a child to learn."

A. "It does no harm to be grateful."

B. "If you think you are too small to make a difference, you haven't spent a night with a mosquito."

C. "The one who forgives ends the argument."

D. "If you close your eyes to facts, you will learn through accidents."

C. "In the moment of crisis, the wise build bridges and the foolish build dams."

D. "Your greatest hope is your greatest fear."

A. "Where there is love there is no darkness."

B. "We wish two things for our children: the first is roots; the second is wings."

C. "Do not tell a child not to touch a hot lamp; the lamp will tell him."

D. "However long the night, the dawn will always break."

A. Don't tell your important secrets to a friend because a friend has other friends.

B. "If you think you have someone eating out of your hands, it is a good idea to count your fingers."

D. "Good words are food; bad words are poison."

A. "A child's face is a child's mirror."

B. "Laughter is a language everyone understands."

C. "Happiness is not perfected until it is shared."

D. "It always seems impossible until it is done."

The proverb that inspired each illustration is listed below in BOLD. However, proverbs and art are always open to interpretation and conversation! When possible, the country of origin of the proverb has been listed.

"There can be no peace without understanding." *Senegal*

"You always learn a lot more when you lose than when you win." *Africa*

"A friend is someone you share the path with." *Sudan*

"There are no shortcuts to the top of the palm tree." *Sierra Leone*

. . .

"When the leg does not walk, the stomach does not eat." *Congo*

"A village without elders is like a well without water." *Uganda*

"A clear conscience makes a soft pillow." *Africa*

"Only once you have carried your own water will you learn the value of every drop." *Namibia*

"A lamp is not valued in the afternoon, but it is valued at night." *Nigeria*

"Wisdom is like a baobab tree; no one individual can embrace it." *Ghana*

"One who is carried on another's back does not appreciate how far off the town is." *Africa*

"A family tie is like a tree; it can bend, but it cannot break." *Africa*

. . .

"Traveling leaves you speechless, then turns you into a storyteller." *Morocco*

"The same sun that melts the wax hardens the clay." *Niger*

"To one who does not know, a small garden is a forest." *Gabon*

"Life is like a shadow and a mist; it passes quickly by and is no more." *Madagascar*

"Hurry, hurry has no blessings."
Mozambique

"You can't chase two antelopes at once." *South Africa*

"Dance in the sun, but turn your back to the clouds." *Zimbabwe*

"A roaring lion kills no game." *Uganda*

. . .

"Restless feet may walk into a snake pit." *Ethiopia*

"Until the lion has his own storyteller, the hunter will always have the best stories." *Zimbabwe*

"A hunter with one arrow does not shoot carelessly." *Kenya*

"Silence has a mighty noise." *Burundi*

. . .

"Those who are at one regarding food are at one in life." *Malawi*

"Beware of time because it has the answers." *Africa*

"Not everyone who chased the zebra caught it, but the one who caught the zebra chased it." *South Africa*

"When the mouse laughs at the cat, there is a hole nearby." *Nigeria*

. . .

"Tomorrow belongs to the people who prepare for it today." *Africa*

"A single bracelet does not jingle."
Congo

"Instruction in youth is like engraving in stone." *Morocco*

"It is not what you call me but what I answer to that matters." *Africa*

"Patience is bitter, but it bears sweet fruit." *Africa*

"If you wait long enough, even an egg will walk." *Ethiopia*

"Nobody is born wise." *Africa*

"You cannot tell a hungry child you gave her food yesterday." *Zimbabwe*

. . .

"Between true friends, even water drunk together is sweet enough." *Africa*

"When spiderwebs unite, they can tie up a lion." *Ethiopia*

"Many hands make light work." *Tanzania*

"Return to old watering holes for more than water: friends and dreams are there to meet you." *Africa*

. . .

"She who learns must teach and she who teaches must learn." *Africa*

"The words of the elders become sweet one day." *Malawi*

"If you wish to move mountains tomorrow, you must start by lifting stones today." *Equatorial Guinea*

"What you help a child to love can be more important than what you help a child to learn." *Africa*

. . .

"It does no harm to be grateful." *Rwanda*

"If you think you are too small to make a difference, you haven't spent a night with a mosquito." *Africa*

"The one who forgives ends the argument." *Africa*

"If you close your eyes to facts, you will learn through accidents." *Africa*

"Traveling is learning." *Kenya*

"Like the turtle, each one of us must stick out our neck if we want to go forward." *Eswatini*

"In the moment of crisis, the wise build bridges and the foolish build dams." *Nigeria*

"Your greatest hope is your greatest fear." *Africa*

. . .

"Where there is love there is no darkness." *Burundi*

"We wish two things for our children: the first is roots; the second is wings." *Sudan*

"Do not tell a child not to touch a hot lamp; the lamp will tell him." *Africa*

"However long the night, the dawn will always break." *Rwanda*

"Don't tell your important secrets to a friend because a friend has other friends." *Africa*

"If you think you have someone eating out of your hands, it is a good idea to count your fingers." *Nigeria*

"Where many are gathered, there is much to be said." *Africa*

"Good words are food; bad words are poison." *Madagascar*

. . .

"A child's face is a child's mirror." *Africa*

"Laughter is a language everyone understands." *Chad*

"Happiness is not perfected until it is shared." *Africa*

"It always seems impossible until it is done." *South Africa*

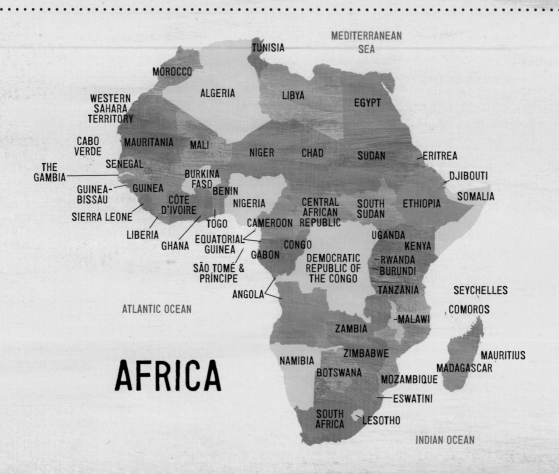

AFRICA